BARB AND DINGBAT'S CRYBABY HOTLINE

BARB AND DINGBAT'S CRYBABY HOTLINE

PATRICK JENNINGS

Holiday House / New York

Library of Congress Cataloging-in-Publication Data
Jennings, Patrick.
Barb and Dingbat's crybaby hotline / Patrick Jennings.—1st ed.
p. cm.
Summary: In the middle 1970s, a junior high school ladies' man and a brainy,
no-nonsense girl engage in verbal combat and soul-baring revelations
through their telephone calls.
ISBN 978-0-8234-2055-1
[1. Telephone calls—Fiction.
2. Interpersonal relations—Fiction.]
I. Title.
PZ7.J4298715Bar 2007
[Fic]—dc22
2006049300

To Bucky,
perfickly flawed

BARB AND DINGBAT'S CRYBABY HOTLINE

1975

[R-R-R-R-RING]

Hello?

Hello, is this Jeff?

Yeah.

Jeff Woolley?

Who's this?

It's not important. I'm just a messenger. I've been asked to inform you that Viv doesn't want to go with you anymore. At all.

But she's supposed to be coming over. I've been waiting here an hour.

I'm sorry. That's the complete message. Thank you for your time.

Who's that laughing?

Laughing?

I hear laughing. It sounds like her.

It's the TV.

It's Viv. I know her voice.

No, you don't. It's Hot Lips Houlihan. I've got M*A*S*H on.

It's Viv.

Hot Lips.

Let me talk to her.

Hot Lips?

Viv.

We must have a bad connection.

You can't hear me?

No, you can't hear *me*.

Stop fooling around, whoever you are, and put her on.

Just a sec.

[silence]

I'm back.

What did she say?

Who?

Who were you talking to?

My cat.

Your *cat*?

I always talk to my cat. Beats talking to most people.

Why couldn't she just call me herself?

She doesn't know your number.

What are you talking about? She calls me all the time!

I ought to know who Dingbat calls. I have to dial for her.

Who's Dingbat?

My cat.

[silence]

Jeff? Are you there?

I'm here.

Are you okay? Are you crying?

No, I'm not crying.

Do you have someone who can hold you in this time of need?

Okay, that was her. I know her snicker.

That was Hot Lips. Now that you say it, though, they do have similar snickers.

Listen, I'll ask you one last time. Put Viv on.

That wasn't asking, and it won't be the last time, I guarantee it.

Why won't she talk to me?

Um, let's see. . . . Because she isn't here?

All right, let's say she isn't there.

That's easy. She isn't here.

What did she do, call you and tell you to call me and tell me she wanted to break up?

Does that seem so strange?

Why didn't she just call me herself?

According to her, she was too busy.

Busy?

She had a date to get ready for.

A *date*?

Forget I said that.

With who? With a *guy*?

No, with her mom. They go out once a week. It's their
way of staying close. They call them dates, just for fun.
Isn't it cute?

Who's the guy? Is it Craig?

Craig Seaman?

Yeah.

He's cute. Icky name, though.

Is it him?

Nope. It's Mom.

[silence]

Uh-oh. More crying. You care deeply for Viv, don't
you, Jeff? This is really, really tearing you up, isn't it?

Knock it off.

I'm sorry. Really I am.

She must have been afraid to call me.

No, too busy. See, she and I were on the phone like five seconds. "Barb," she says, "call Jeff and drop him for me, will you, sweetie?"

Barb? Barb Grimaldi? Is that who this is?

And I say, "Sure, honey. Consider it done." You and I have been on the phone ten minutes already and you're still in the denial phase. You still have to get through depression, anger, and begging before you get to acceptance. Those are the five stages of grief, you know: denial, depression, anger, begging, and acceptance.

Did she say why?

Why what?

Why she's dropping me?

Acceptance. That's a good sign. But she isn't *dropping* you. The dropping is over. You've been *dropped*, man.

There, *that* was her.

Hot Lips again.

Put her on the phone!

Anger. You're regressing.

Put . . . her . . . *on*!

Okay, okay. Don't have a conniption. I'll get her.

About time!

[silence]

Viv?

[silence]

Viv? Is that you?

[silence]

There. Satisfied?

She didn't say anything.

She never does. Dingbat doesn't like the phone. She finds it impersonal.

You're enjoying this, aren't you?

What?

Screwing with my head.

Yes.

You know what, Barb? You're a real ballbuster.

And you have a nice day, too. Buh-bye.

[CLICK]

[R-R-R-R-RING]

Thank you for calling Barb and Dingbat's Crybaby Hotline. All our counselors are currently handling other whiners. Please hold for a shoulder to cry on.

Very funny.

Well, if it isn't Mr. Jeffrey Pottymouth. What a delightful surprise. How'd you get this number?

You're in the book. Grimaldi, Barbara. You have your own line, don't you?

What of it?

Look. All I want is to talk to Viv, okay? *Please?*

We're begging now. Excellent.

I'm not begging. I'm asking nicely.

She's on a date with her mom. Do you need a diagram?

Come on, Barb. Have a heart.

No thanks. I have one. And besides, I don't think you have much to spare.

Fine. Whatever. I don't care.

Uh-oh.

What?

Depression.

You _could_ show some feeling, you know.

I'm nothing but feeling. I was awarded a Girl Scout badge for feeling.

Do you ever mean anything you say?

I always say exactly what I mean.

Which means you don't. I don't think you've said one truthful thing since you picked up the phone.

That's not fair, Jeff. I really do have a cat named Dingbat. And I really am watching M*A*S*H. And Viv really did drop you.

Since when is _M*A*S*H_ on Saturday night?

It's a special two-part episode, because of Veterans Day.

It's not on. I checked. You're lying. And you're lying about Viv not being there laughing at all your dumb lies.

Really?

Really. And I think that sucks because she's dropping me and I don't even get to talk to her about it. I just get jerked around by her smart-ass friend.

Meaning me?

Meaning you.

Those are some serious charges there, Mr. Woolley. I hope you've got some solid evidence to back them up. Otherwise you could have a slander suit on your hands.

Viv isn't on a date with Craig or her mom or anyone else. She's at your house listening to you jerk me around.

This is amazing. I've never talked to an actual paranoid schizophrenic before.

You're going to keep on lying?

That really hurts, Jeff. I only called you because Viv's

my friend and she needed my help. I have no reason to lie to you. I barely even know you.

Barely even know me? Are you crazy? We've *kissed*.

You and I? Why don't I remember that?

Stop messing around. You know. Last summer, at the pool, behind the Coke machine.

You've got the wrong girl there, Jeffrey. I'm positive I've never kissed anyone behind a beverage dispenser before, and I've certainly never kissed you, anyplace. I'm not even sure I know what you look like. Don't you have terrible skin and no lips?

It's kind of fun talking to you. It's like a game show. If I can get you to say one true thing, I win.

You've already won. I am a fountain of truth.

We kissed.

To quote Aerosmith: "Dream on."

You were wearing a yellow string bikini. And your breath tasted like nachos.

I've never, nor will I ever, own a string bikini, and the

last thing in the world I'd be caught dead eating would be the cheese they serve at the pool. "Cheese food." What is that? What cheese eats?

It wasn't a big deal. I got one of those notes in the hall: "Do you like Barb? Yes or no. Circle one." I circled "yes." Then I bumped into you when I came out of the showers that day at the pool. We talked awhile, then went behind the Coke machine and made out. So what?

That's so romantic. I wonder who the girl was?

Then on Monday I got this note saying you were breaking up with me.

Not much luck with the ladies, I see.

Hot Lips again.

No. Dingbat. Hair ball.

Can we change the game?

Game?

Instead of me asking you questions and you lying, how about you lie and I'll give you the question?

Like *Jeopardy.*

Right.

But I never lie.

Okay, then say something true and I'll give you the question.

Oh, I don't know. I'm not very good at games.

I wouldn't say that.

All right, I'll give it a try. Let me think.

[silence]

Okay, here's one: Paranoid schizophrenics often believe others to be liars.

Why are you lying about Viv not being there?

This is fun. Here's another one: There's never anything to do in this town.

Why do you lie all the time?

You're not as dumb as I thought.

Do you think Viv dropped me because I don't have lips?

You have some lips.

Why did you kiss me behind the Coke machine?

Are we still playing?

You are. Now give the phone to Viv, you jerk!

[CLICK]

[R-R-R-R-RING]

Schizophrenics Anonymous. To which of your personalities do I have the pleasure of speaking?

Is Viv really on a date with some guy?

You want Paranoiacs Anonymous. I'll connect you.

Did you have anything to do with it?

Maybe you want Lobotomies "R" Us. We can send someone right over with a drill.

What did you tell her about me?

"Delusions of grandeur," they call this. What makes you think I've ever so much as spoken your name before?

Because you made out with me behind the Coke machine.

Obsessive-compulsive, too. You're really a mess, son.

Where do you get all your bull crap?

Talk shows. Where do you get yours?

I think you know why Viv doesn't want to go with me anymore.

Psychic as well as psycho?

You're her friend. She'd tell you.

And if she did, would she want me to tell you?

No. But I can keep a secret. Unless she's there, she'll never know I know.

And I should believe that? I should betray my friend to someone who talks to my cat on the phone?

I think you had something to do with it.

With what?

With Viv dropping me. You wanted to be the one who told me. You like hurting people.

Really?

You're the one that's psycho, man. You're Looney Tunes.

"Th-that's all, f-f-folks!"

[CLICK]

[R-R-R-R-RING]

Fudd Wesidence.

Look, I don't know what's going on or why you're doing this or why Viv is dropping me, but, you know what, I don't care anymore. At. All. Just do me one thing, okay, Barb? If you see Viv, tell her to drop dead.

Oh, I can't remember anything unless I write it down. Let me get a pencil. Hold, please.

Knock it off, Barb. Barb?

Okay, got one. "Jeff . . . says . . . drop—" I'm sorry. How'd that go again?

Drop. Dead.

[CLICK]

[R-R-R-R-RING]

Hello?

Good evening, sir. Do I have the pleasure of speaking to Jeffrey Woolley?

Yes.

This is Francesca Umbilini from *Tiger Beat* magazine. We're conducting a readers' poll and wondered whether or not you'd be willing to answer a few questions.

Sure, go ahead.

Great! First question: Have you been dropped in the last twenty-four hours?

As a matter of fact, yes, I have.

Wonderful. On a scale from one to ten, then, how would you rate your current feelings of rejection, with one being "deeply wounded" and ten being "devastated"?

Zero.

You're clever. We at *Tiger Beat* like that. We know teenagers are a lot more on the ball than adults give them credit for. But seriously, with heartbreak this fresh, you must be doubled over in pain. We sympathize. All of us here at *Tiger Beat* were teenagers once ourselves, you know.

Congratulations.

Ha, ha! You *are* clever. Now, the next question is multiple choice. Please complete the following: The reason my ex-girlfriend dropped me was because: a) I have no lips, b) I have no personality, c) I have a pizza face, or d) all of the above.

I don't know why she dropped me.

You don't?

No. She sicced this head-tripping friend of hers on me, and I can't get a straight answer out of her.

How despicable! Why don't you confront your ex directly?

She's at the head-tripping friend's house, though the head-tripping friend keeps denying it.

My, how childish! It sounds to me like maybe you're better off, Jeffrey.

That's what I'm starting to think.

And that friend can't be a very nice person, either.

I don't know her very well, but I do think she enjoys watching other people suffer.

Suffer? Oh dear. You *are* suffering, aren't you, Jeff?

No, I'm not, which must be why she calls and pretends she's someone else.

[CLICK]

[R-R-R-R-RING]

You haven't reached the Sarcasm Connection. All of our lines aren't busy. So don't hold, because no one will be with you shortly.

Well! We're seeing a whole new side to Mr. Jeffrey Woollybutt, aren't we? Maybe Mr. Jeffrey Woollybutt isn't as mopey as everyone says. *Maybe* Mr. Jeffrey Woollybutt even has a teensy-weensy sense of humor.

Who says I'm mopey?

Did I say mopey? I meant charismatic.

I don't think I'm mopey.

And that's what counts.

What does "mopey" mean, anyway?

Self-pitying. Sulky. Slouchy.

I don't slouch.

Of course you don't. Your posture is perfect, like Miss America's.

Will you knock it off?

You don't like beauty pageants? I understand. They objectify women and all that women's lib stuff. I can think of a lot of better ways to judge people than lining them up in string bikinis.

I bet you can.

Come again?

I bet you can think of lots of ways to judge people.

Are you implying that I'm judgmental, Mr. Woolly-butt? Because if you are, I'd like to remind you it wasn't I who called someone Looney Tunes.

No, you said I was psycho.

That wasn't a judgment. That was a diagnosis.

And mopey. You called me mopey.

No, that was *everyone*. *Everyone* calls you mopey. And besides, I corrected myself. I meant charismatic.

I'm not sure I know what that means.

People with true charisma don't. That's how you know you've got it.

Well, I don't care what people think. If they think I'm mopey, then they just haven't taken the time to get to know me.

That's the spirit.

Just because I don't belong to some group or something.

You obviously dance to your own drummer.

I just don't understand why everybody talks about the things they talk about all the time.

What else can they talk about?

I don't know. Something else.

They should talk about something other than what they can talk about?

They could talk about something besides TV. Or who's going with who. Or who dropped who.

That's all beneath you.

No. I talk about it sometimes.

So the problem is . . .

I just wish people could talk about other things sometimes, that's all.

For example?

You'll just make fun of me.

Ah, you don't trust me. And after all we've been through. That hurts, Jeff.

See?

How 'bout I guess?

Guess?

I'll guess what everyone should be talking about, and if I get it right, I get a prize.

What sort of prize?

Nothing too expensive. I'll leave it up to you.

There isn't a right answer.

Sure there is. Let me guess. Watergate? Agent Orange? Skyjacking? Inflation? Starving children in Africa?

Keep going. I love hearing the problems of the world turned into a joke.

A joke? You think I think starving children are funny? What kind of monster do you think I am?

I don't know. What kind of monster are you?

Not the kind that laughs at starving children.

So what do you think of starving children?

I think they should be fed. Don't you?

It wouldn't be funny if you were the one who was starving.

What do you mean *funny*? You think I'm being *funny*? What are *you* doing? You think a bunch of teenagers discussing starving African children in the halls at Indianola Junior High is going to *do* something?

I never said we should discuss it in the halls.

You don't want it discussed in the halls?

I'd love it discussed in the halls. At least it'd be better than discussing what everyone's wearing.

What are you wearing?

Shut up.

So you're saying everyone's shallow?

Not everyone.

Everyone but you?

No.

You're obviously very deep.

I'm not saying I'm deep or that anyone is shallow. I just wish sometimes I'd be surprised by what I hear people talking about. Don't you get bored by what they talk about?

I like talking about TV. TV's great. There are many programs worthy of long, in-depth discussion. Like *Welcome Back, Kotter.*

You're being sarcastic again.

I'm never sarcastic.

***That's* sarcastic.**

You don't love *Welcome Back, Kotter?* The way Barbarino never knows anything, the way he goes, "What? Where? When?" and "Up your nose with a rubber hose?" And Horshack going, "Ooh-ooh! Ooh-ooh!" every time he raises his hand. This is classic comedy right up there with *Gilligan's Island* and *Mister Ed.*

You're not being serious.

I'm *dead* serious. My life is better because of *Welcome Back, Kotter.* And I don't mind at all that the main characters are guys. Or that the only girl on the show is a slut.

Hotsy Totsy.

So you *do* watch.

I've seen it. I think it's dumb, and so do you.

Of course I do. Everyone does. That's why we watch it. It makes us feel smarter than the adults who write it.

I don't know about that. I think a lot of people really think it's funny. I hear guys saying "Up your nose with a rubber hose" all the time.

"What? Where? When?"

Glenn McComb got sent to the office for saying that in Volker's class. He got detention for a week.

Teachers don't get our humor. Volker probably doesn't even watch *Kotter.* He probably watches PBS.

And that's bad?

That's bad. PBS is like school.

And school is bad?

Very bad.

What would you do if you didn't have to go to school?

I don't know. Watch more TV.

Don't you do anything besides go to school and watch TV?

Don't you?

I asked you.

I asked *you*.

Yeah, I do other things. I don't watch much TV.

Me either. The boob tube. What a waste of time.

You just said if you didn't have to go to school, you'd watch more.

I would.

But then you said it's a waste of time.

I like wasting time.

Why?

What else is there to do? Drag girls behind beverage dispensers? Build toy boats?

Viv told you about my boats?

Everyone knows about the boats, Jeff.

What's wrong with building model ships?

Nothing. I'm sure it's very rewarding. And practical. And fun. And the glue sure explains a lot. What do you do with them after they're built? Play with them in the tub?

No. They're not seaworthy.

Not seaworthy. I see.

They're just for display. I keep them on a shelf in my room.

How many are there?

I don't know.

More than a hundred? Less than a million?

Less than a million.

It's good to know you haven't been wasting your life.

And what do you do that's so important, besides watching TV and dropping your girlfriends' boyfriends for them?

I eat right and take my Geritol every morning.

Wait a minute—I did *not* drag you behind the Coke machine.

That's right. You didn't.

You *wanted* to go back there. You even used your *tongue*.

I did? I can't imagine what for.

If anything, *you* dragged *me*.

What an interesting accusation, considering I wasn't even there.

Why can't you admit it? There's nothing wrong with it. It was just kissing.

According to you, it was just French kissing.

So, what's wrong with that?

Nothing, I guess. If you're French. Or a slut.

Only Hotsy Totsys make out, is that it?

Something like that.

You think making out with me means you're a slut?

Making out with you would mean I'm insane.

Oh, forget it. I don't know why I'm wasting my time talking to you.

Ditto.

[CLICK]

[R-R-R-R-RING]

Yeah? Now what?

Uh . . . hello? Is Jeff there?

Look, Barb, I really can't talk anymore. I can't be on the phone after nine.

Um . . . Jeff? This is Dee.

Dee?

Dee Rigo. You know . . . from school?

Dee? I'm sorry. I thought you were someone else.

If you can't talk . . .

No. Yeah. I can talk. For a minute anyway. Since you called and everything.

Why can't you talk after nine?

My grandparents. It's nothing. Never mind.

35

I wouldn't want to get you into trouble with your gram and gramps.

Very funny. You had me for a minute.

Sorry?

No, it's you. I'm hanging up.

Um . . . I'll call another time, Jeff. You sound pretty, uh . . . freaked out.

How 'bout you give me your number and I'll call you back another time.

Are you stoned or something?

Just give me your number.

I don't think I'm going to do that, Jeff. You're in a weird mood.

Uh-huh. Just as I thought . . . *Barb*.

Well, I'll let you go now, Jeff. See you at school on Wednesday. Have a nice holiday.

[CLICK]

[R-R-R-R-RING]

I am Barbara. Hear me roar.

Why'd you do that?

Might I ask to whom I am speaking?

Why'd you pretend to be Dee Rigo?

I, Dee Rigo?

Don't play dumb. You called and pretended you were Dee.

What? Where? When?

You called and you know you called.

I'm watching *Mary Tyler Moore*. Did you know that she can take a nothing day and suddenly make it all seem worthwhile? Kinda like you, Jeff.

I don't have time for any of your bull crap.

Why? Important engagement? Annual meeting of the Association of Toy-Boat Nerds?

I told you. It's my grandparents.

Your grandparents?

I just can't be on the phone now.

But Jeffrey, dear, you *are* on the phone now.

Just to tell you not to call anymore.

You called to tell me not to call you?

I called you *back* to tell you not to.

You're really coming unglued over there, aren't you, buddy? Want me to call a paramedic? Or maybe those guys with the jackets with the really long sleeves?

Why Dee Rigo? Why did you pretend to be *her*?

Exactly. Why in the name of Gilligan would I pretend to be Dee Rigo? And how does one even go about pretending to be Dee Rigo? Talk real fluttery? Flirt real hard?

You think Dee is flirtatious?

Is the Fonz cool?

I don't really know her.

You know her.

What're you talking about?

I mean, she's not a tough nut to crack.

She's never called me before. I've only ever talked to her for something like two minutes in my life.

A lot can happen in two minutes.

What does that mean?

Better lower your voice, Jeffy. You'll wake your gram and gramps.

***There*, see? That's just what you said when you were being Dee. I don't even call my grandparents that. I call them Pops and Nana.**

Pops and Nana. Quaint.

No more phone calls, okay? I'm sick of your head games.

[CLICK]

[R-R-R-R-RING]

It's nine-twenty. Do you know where your grandparents are?

I want you to tell me it was you.

It was me.

You called and pretended to be Dee, right?

Aren't you calling a little late? Where are Pops and Nana?

Just answer the question.

Which was . . . ?

Oh, forget it. I'll never get a straight answer out of you.

You really are upset, aren't you, Jeffy? Tell Barb all about it.

I just want to know if it was you pretending to be Dee.

Because if it wasn't, it might really have been Dee, is that it? And Dee you'd like to hear from? Am I on the right track, Tonto?

It wasn't her. It was you.

What did you do, accuse her of being me? Ha!

You know I did.

Well, she knows now.

Knows what?

Knows what the rest of us know: You don't have all your oars in the water, Admiral Toyboat.

It wasn't her.

You sure about that?

It couldn't have been.

Why don't you call her back?

What if it wasn't her?

I wouldn't worry about that. She's probably heard through the grapevine you're available. She's freshly single herself, and she's a rebound girl from way back. She'll love hearing from you.

You said she probably thinks I'm crazy.

So what? What boy isn't?

What am I talking about? It was *you*. *You* called.

Why would I walk away from Mary and the gang just to call you and pretend to be some hot-to-trot drum majorette? What *is* a majorette, anyway? Sounds like some kind of cookie.

Swear on the Bible you didn't pretend to be Dee.

Okay. I solemnly swear I didn't call you and pretend to be Dee Rigo.

You probably have something crossed.

Yes, Jeffrey. My *eyes* are crossed. You're driving me nuts.

If I call her and she didn't call me, I'm calling you right back.

Threats, threats. Listen to some advice, Jeff. I'm okay; you're not. This breakup has really hit you hard. Take some time to be by yourself, just *you* and *you*. Don't rush into another relationship. That wouldn't be fair, to you or to Dee. Take this time to do a little soul-searching. Try to find yourself.

Talk-show advice?

Mr. Kotter.

[CLICK]

[R-R-R-R-RING]

Barb Grimaldi, impersonator for hire. Barbra Streisand, Kate Hepburn, Dee Rigo—I do them all.

She wasn't home.

She's probably on her way over. I'd brush my teeth.

Her mom said she's out bowling with some friends.

I love bowling. It's so kinky sharing shoes with the whole filthy world.

She couldn't have called me. It was you.

Do you ever bowl, Mr. Woolley? Have you ever been to Shady Lanes? They have this incredible machine there. Pong, it's called. It's right next to the *pay phone.*

I think I would've been able to tell if she was calling from a bowling alley, don't you?

Slow night?

It's Saturday.

So maybe she's not at the bowling alley. Are you always where your parents think you are?

[silence]

Jeffrey?

I'm here.

Do your parents always know where you are? Are you some sort of goody-goody or something?

I never tell them anything. They're dead.

What? *Really?*

Really.

What happened?

None of your business.

Right. Of course. Sorry. I mean, really I—I'm sorry.

Skip it.

[silence]

So you live with your grandparents?

Yeah. Pops and Nana. You want to make fun of them again?

I didn't make fun of them. I just said their names were quaint.

They're quaint people.

I'm sure they are. God. I feel just awful, Jeff.

It's not a big thing. They died a long time ago, when I was little.

How?

Car accident.

They were together?

Yeah.

How old were you?

Four.

And your grandparents raised you?

Yeah.

My parents are both alive. Technically, anyway.

[silence]

46

Come on, Jeff, help me out here. I don't know what to say to this. I've never met a real live orphan before.

Why don't you start by telling me the truth about Viv.

The truth?

Why she dropped me.

What difference does it make? Girls drop boys every day. Do they have to have a reason? Do you think knowing is going to help you somehow? I guarantee you it won't.

So you *know* why.

I know the little bit she bothered to say about it. It's not like she bared her soul to me or anything. It's not that big a deal to her.

So then tell me.

First you tell me something. What made you go with her in the first place?

What do you mean?

I mean, what did you like about her?

Like about her? I didn't really know her.

Another "circle one" note?

Yeah.

How many of those notes do you get?

I used to get a lot.

Why?

I don't know.

Yes you do.

Because I'm on the team?

And you're cute.

I am?

Don't pretend you don't know.

I guess people have said it before.

Girls have, you mean.

Like *guys* would. And, actually, girls have told me *other* girls said I was cute.

Have you ever circled "no"?

Of course! I'm not *desperate.*

Do you kiss all the yeses?

Pretty much. I like making out.

Do they all break up with you?

So far. I mean, I'm not married or anything.

Why do they drop you?

I've dropped a few myself.

Why did you start going with Viv?

She asked me to. She's a fox. I wanted to make out with her.

And you don't know why they all drop you?

You said girls don't need reasons.

I said they usually don't have them, but they always claim to. Usually they're more like excuses: "He's short," "He's dumb," "He smells weird."

Do I smell weird?

I wouldn't know.

Yes you would.

No I wouldn't.

What excuse did Viv give?

All she told me was you were a drag.

A drag?

A drag.

What'd she mean by that?

I don't know. Don't you?

Well, I didn't like hanging out with her friends.

They only talked about TV and who's going with who?

Yeah.

You're sounding pretty antisocial, Mr. Woolley.

And she always wanted to talk on the phone.

So?

I hate talking on the phone.

Obviously.

I mean, she never really talked about anything interesting.

What's on TV and who's going with who?

Mostly who's going with who.

She said something else, too, but I don't know if I should tell you.

I hate when people tell you they have a secret but they don't know if they should tell you. I think they're dying to tell you.

I'm not dying. I don't want to be the one that has to tell a poor orphan he can't kiss.

She said I can't kiss?

Not exactly.

What'd she say?

She said you kiss like a maniac.

What does that mean?

You don't know?

Do I kiss like a maniac?

How would I know?

Come on, tell me.

I have nothing to tell.

You're going to keep denying it?

You're going to keep imagining it?

"Kiss like a maniac." What does that *mean*?

You have no idea?

I like kissing. Maybe she meant I kissed her too much?

How often did you kiss her?

I don't know. Whenever we were together.

You mean whenever you were *alone* together?

We weren't always alone.

You kissed her in front of other people?

Sometimes. Is that wrong?

Not necessarily. Who did you kiss her in front of? The principal? Her parents? Her priest?

Just in front of normal people.

Where'd you kiss her?

What do you mean?

I certainly don't mean where on her person did you kiss her, Jeffrey, and so please kindly refrain from sharing any details of that sort with me or I will definitely become violently ill.

We kissed in the halls. In the gym. Behind the gym. In the parking lot. At the bus stop. In the cafeteria.

Don't you know that kissing on school grounds is strictly forbidden? You're lucky you weren't expelled.

So you think that's what she meant by "maniac"? That I kissed her too much?

I'm not sure. *How* did you kiss her?

What do you mean?

Do you close your eyes?

I can't believe you're asking me that. You *know*.

Just answer the question, Pinocchio.

You know I do.

You never peek? Just to be sure you're kissing the right girl?

Huh?

Skip it. So what're you thinking about when you're kissing all these girls?

Thinking about?

Yeah, what's on your *mind*—you know, that squishy thing between your ears?

I don't know what I think of. Nothing, really. Just kissing, I guess. You're not supposed to think when you're making out, are you?

You don't think about, say, how much you like the girl whose lips you're mashing?

Well, yeah, I'm thinking that.

Each time? Each girl?

You getting at something?

I guess I'm wondering if sometimes all those lips don't blur together.

You mean, do I ever forget who I'm kissing?

Maybe.

Of course I don't! What do you think I am?

I have no idea what you are, but you make it sound as if you're some kind of kissaholic who doesn't really care who he's making out with so long as he's making out.

That's not true. I always know who I'm making out with.

Do you ever talk to a girl first? Do you ever get to know her before you start tasting her tongue?

What's it to you? Where do you get off asking me this stuff?

Well, I am a friend of Viv's, not to mention Pammi Tinling's, and Marla Blagdon's, and Tina Kasicki's.

I never kissed Marla Blagdon.

Last year, at the Sadie Hawkins dance. She asked you to go. You kissed her sixteen times during "(Hey, Won't You Play) Another Somebody Done Somebody Wrong Song."

She counted?

You weren't on the dance floor, of course. You were hiding behind the folded-up lunch tables.

I hate dances.

It was the first time she'd ever kissed a boy. She had a crush on you for over a year. I had to practically twist her arm to get her to ask you. She was too afraid to do it in person, so she sent a note. You circled "yes."

I honestly don't remember kissing her.

You went with her for a week. She said you kissed her every chance you got. Then she broke up with you because you kept pressuring her to let you go to second base. Oh, how I hate baseball metaphors for sex.

You're making this all up. I never kissed Marla.

How about Dee Rigo? Did you ever kiss her?

I told you, I don't really know her.

What do you mean, "really"?

I mean, I kind of know her from school. She's in my health class. But I've never talked to her or anything.

You never talk to any girl. It's the "anything" I wonder about.

Why don't you ever just come out and say what you mean?

Have you ever kissed Dee Rigo?

I told you I didn't.

You didn't say you didn't. You said you didn't really know her.

How can I kiss her if I don't know her?

That's what I'd like to know.

Are you saying I *did* kiss her?

I'm not saying anything.

I never kissed Dee Rigo.

Or Marla Blagdon.

Or Marla Blagdon. What is this?

I saw you kiss Marla between the lunch tables. And I saw you kiss Dee Rigo behind the Coke machine at the pool.

Oh, *now* I get it! I didn't kiss *you* behind the Coke machine. I kissed *Dee.* You're crazy!

Pipe down, there, grandchild. Old people need their sleep.

I kissed *you* behind the Coke machine, Barb. Why can't you admit it?

Tell me something. What do I look like?

What?

What do I *look* like?

I know what you look like.

So tell me.

Tell you what? What color your hair is? How tall you are?

Right. I'm Dirty Harry, and I'm really steamed, punk. You better talk, punk, if you know what's good for ya.

Why?

Cops don't have to say why, punk. Just give me a description. And none a' your lip.

Well, you're kinda, I don't know, average.

Average for what? Average for a white girl in an American junior high school? Average for a *pretty* white girl in an American junior high school? Average for a *fat*, pretty white girl in an American junior high school?

Just average. Not fat or skinny. Not tall. Not short. Not ugly—

A fox.

So you're just fishing for compliments—

No, I'm trying to figure out how you distinguish between the girls you kiss.

What are you talking about? Every girl looks different.

How are Dee and I different?

You just are. You're different girls. You have different faces.

Does my hair have a particular color, or is it average, too?

It's brown.

Light brown? Dark brown?

Medium brown.

So I'm Jane Doe.

Who's Jane Doe?

Someone you haven't kissed. Do I have an eye color?

I'm sure you do.

Remember which?

No.

You allege that you kissed me. That means you were pretty darn close to my face. You didn't notice the color of my eyes?

Maybe I did. I just don't remember. It was last summer.

Dinosaurs roamed the earth.

Are they brown?

Sure they're not blue?

Yeah, I remember now. They're blue.

Or purple?

No, they're blue.

What else do you remember? Any scars? Beauty marks? Moles? Zits?

I didn't notice anything like that.

You didn't notice my appendix scar? After all, I was wearing a string bikini. Or the mark where I got my polio shot? Do I wear braces? Or glasses?

You don't wear glasses. Do you? I mean, you weren't wearing any that day.

Surely you'd remember braces. You did kiss me.

No braces. I'm positive of that.

Okay. So let's see what we've got so far: medium height, medium weight, medium brown hair, possibly blue eyes, no glasses, no braces, no distinguishing marks. I doubt the artist's rendering would result in an arrest. Now how about a description of Dee Rigo.

Why?

I just want to see if you're as bad an eyewitness as I think.

She's pretty average, too.

Really? Who isn't average?

I'm tired of this game. I want to know why you pretended to be Dee.

I want to know why you pretended Dee was me.

What?

Do you think we look alike?

You and Dee?

Does she wear braces?

No.

I do.

You *do*?

[silence]

Did you last summer?

Since sixth grade.

I didn't notice.

Is Dee medium height?

No, she's kind of tall. Taller than you. And her hair is darker. Almost black.

Dee sits in front of me in algebra. I can see right over her head, which is covered with dishwater blond hair. Not darker than mine. Mine's black.

You're lying. And you don't wear braces, either. I'd remember.

Because you kissed me.

Because we *Frenched*.

And you never lie.

Right.

You and Dick Nixon.

I don't lie.

So where are your parents, George Washington? In their graves, or were they cremated? Or maybe they're just in Baltimore? Maybe at a wedding?

[silence]

Viv told you?

That's why you wanted her to come over. You said you had the house to yourself all weekend. You were planning on rounding first and sliding into second. Or maybe stretching it into a triple? Or were you going to attempt an inside-the-park home run?

You pretended to be Dee. I figured, since you lie, why can't I?

So you kill your parents.

I didn't kill them. I was joking.

Funny as a crutch, Jeff.

I wanted to stop you from being sarcastic for a minute. You wouldn't give me a straight answer about anything.

Is there really a Pops and Nana?

They live in Nebraska.

And you call me a liar.

It was one lie. You've been lying all night.

I have not.

You said you were watching *M*A*S*H.* You said Viv wasn't there. By the way, is she still there?

She never was.

At least when I get caught, I admit it.

You haven't caught me in anything. You're just making accusations based on circumstantial evidence.

You pretended to be Dee.

Circumstantial.

Oh, come on! Why don't you just admit it? It was *you.*

It wasn't.

Then at least admit I kissed you. That's not circumstantial. I was there, remember? I'm an eyewitness. You were there. We *kissed.*

We didn't.

Man! You drive me crazy!

So hang up. Why are you still on the phone? This has got to be the longest conversation you've ever had with a girl you haven't Frenched. What is it you want from me anyhow? Why do you keep calling me?

I don't know.

[silence]

I guess I was thinking I'd ask if you wanted to go together.

Go together! You don't even know who I am.

What do you mean? You're Barb.

That's right. Barb Grimaldi. Grimaldi is an Italian name, in case you don't know. I have dark black, not "medium brown," hair on my head, and on my arms and legs, too, unfortunately. And I have a little black mustache, which I'm not too happy about, and which I destroy every week or so with Nair. I wear braces that stick out of my mouth half a mile. My eyes are black, not blue. I'm not medium height. I'm tall. Taller than Dee Rigo, taller than most of the boys on the basketball team, including you. I'm not medium weight. I'm a five-foot-nine-inch toothpick with a mouth full of metal, hair on my arms, and a mustache. Does that ring a bell? I'd be quite a sight in a string bikini, if I ever wore one, which I never have, or will.

[silence]

I've never gone with a girl taller than me. Kissing would be weird.

Bingo.

Wait a minute. . . .

I can hear that thing between your ears going squish, squish. . . .

So who did I make out with at the pool?

Dee has a yellow string bikini.

I kissed Dee Rigo?

Right behind the Coke machine.

But wait. When I came out of the showers, *you* came up to me.

Dee came up to you.

But I was supposed to meet *you* at the pool.

I was there.

And I kissed Dee?

You tell me. Did you kiss a short dishwater blonde with great teeth or a hairy beanpole with a hamster cage in her mouth?

[silence]

It *was* Dee. She came up to me and said, "Feeling better?" and I said, "Was I feeling bad?" And she said she meant the shower. We started talking about how disgusting the bathrooms were and I noticed she was really flirting with me.

Dee Rigo, flirting? What a shock.

I remember she kept touching me when she talked. Then she kind of pulled me behind the Coke machine and we made out.

I know. I had a poolside seat.

But I thought it was you. How can that be?

She was a girl. What's in a name? Did you even know what I looked like when you circled "yes"?

I don't really remember.

We'd never met before.

Then why'd you send me the note?

I didn't. Tina Kasicki did.

Tina Kasicki?

One of your former kissing posts. There are a lot of them at Indianola.

I haven't gone with *that* many girls.

No more than Hugh Hefner.

I sure haven't gone with many this year.

You have a rep now.

What do you mean?

You make out with every girl with lips, and pretty soon they get wise. Girls like to believe that when they're being kissed, the kisser actually knows who they're kissing.

I know who I'm kissing.

Tell that to Dee Rigo. She didn't know it, but when she was making out with you behind the beverage dispenser, she was me.

She was a good kisser.

Too bad she dropped you.

You dropped me!

It was my pleasure.

[silence]

Okay, so I kissed Dee. I screwed up. But that was last summer. What about tonight? Want to come over?

Did you drop acid or something?

Come on over. There's no one here. My parents left an open bottle of sherry in the fridge. We have a twenty-five-inch color TV. Solid-state. Let me make it up to you.

Make it up to me?

I owe you one. For making out with Dee.

You don't owe me anything.

I said I'd go with you. I circled "yes."

I dropped you, remember?

But we never actually went together.

We never said a word to each other.

So now we have. We can start over.

No thanks.

Why not?

Tina passed you that note without asking me. I told her once I thought you were kind of cute and I actually liked how awkward and shy you seemed. I can be awkward and shy, too.

Hard to believe.

Yeah, well, talking on the phone's different than talking to real live people. No one can see your braces. Or your mustache.

Yeah.

I was mad at Tina when she told me about the note, but then she told me you wanted to go with me, and, I have to admit, I was a little excited. I'd never gone with anyone. I'd never been asked. Blame the mustache. But I was also pretty terrified. I'd never said so much as boo to you before. I worried you'd be just another dumb boy who only cares about cars and sports and yourself. Marla said you weren't like that. She said you barely talked at all, that mostly you guys just made out. I saw that as a challenge. I'd make you talk. I'd draw you out. And I didn't mind the thought of making out with you. Like I said, I thought you were pretty cute.

Come on over, then. Now you know I'm not just another dumb boy who talks about cars and sports.

Right. Now I know you're a dumb boy who thinks all girls are the same, that we're all just pairs of lips to be mashed.

That's not—

Now I know you think you're above the rest of us and our shallow TV talk and gossip. You're not shy. You're sitting back judging everyone. And I also know you're desperate enough to invite a girl over even when you couldn't pick her out of a line up. I know you a *lot* better now, Jeffrey Woolley, and I am circling "no."

[silence]

Look, Jeff, I'm sorry I said all that. I barely know you.

Maybe I deserve it. Maybe you're right.

Oh, I am, but that doesn't mean I have the right to say it.

I think I'll hang up now. My ear is numb.

Mine too.

[silence]

I'm really sorry, Dee.

Barb! *Jerk!*

[CLICK]

1976

[R-R-R-R-RING]

Hello?

Hi, Jeff. It's Barb. We need to talk. Meg was here.

What? *Meg*?

Collect yourself, now, chum. She was here, with me, at my house. Got it?

But *why*?

She came over to talk about tonight. Do you remember tonight?

She was *there*?

Breathe now.

She told *you*?

You're going to be all right.

I've been looking for her everywhere. Why did she go to *your* house?

She figured you wouldn't look here. And she figured right. She says she knows you and I talk a lot.

And she told you what happened?

Yes.

What does she want you to tell me?

I think you know.

She doesn't want to go with me anymore?

Bingo.

Where is she?

On her way home. She said she'd talk to you later, when you're calm.

I *am* calm.

She wants to stay your friend. She likes you.

Likes?

That's nothing to sneeze at, Jeff.

But we've been going together for over *three weeks*.

I understand, and I'm sorry. Really I am.

Why are you being so nice all of a sudden? You're the

one who calls her a dumb cheerleader. "Little Miss Backflip."

That was wrong. I didn't know her. Sometimes, I admit, I can be a tad judgmental.

A *tad*?

She's a delightful person. I see why you like her so much. Now you need to behave yourself so you can keep her as a friend.

I'm going to go over there.

No, you're not. You're going to turn on the TV and watch something mindless. It shouldn't be too hard to find.

There's nothing on but news.

Perfect. Watch that. Get some perspective. Or build a boat. Just stop worrying about where your next kiss is coming from. And listen up, pal: You are not to go to Meg's. You are not to call her. Or me. Is that perfectly clear?

Can I come over to your house?

No. Good night, Jeffrey.

[CLICK]

[R-R-R-R-RING]

Grimaldi Institute for the Hard of Hearing. I say, *GRIMALDI INSTITUTE FOR THE HARD OF HEARING!*

It's me again.

You *are* hard of hearing. Did you not hear me say you are not to call me?

I tried not to.

Try harder.

[CLICK]

[R-R-R-R-RING]

Grimaldi Institute for the Hard of *Heeding.* Mr. Woolley, leave your handset in its cradle. Krazy Glue it there if you have to.

I tried Meg. Her line's busy.

Not busy. Off the hook. Unlike you.

What'd I do that was so horrible?

Pretending you don't know will only make it worse.

What does that mean?

Then again, maybe you really don't remember. You have a tendency to repress unpleasant memories.

Skip the talk-show bull crap, Babs.

You mauled Meg by the trophy case.

Mauled? She said "mauled"?

She was more charitable. She said you suddenly came at her with "Russian" hands and "Roman" fingers.

That sounds more like her.

But it was mauling, all right. If she's describing it accurately, you broke several state laws and a couple of federal ones, not to mention the Indianola Junior High School Student Code of Conduct.

I broke federal laws?

You broke *universal* laws, Woolboy.

For instance?

For instance, "A teenager shall not invade the sanctity of another teenager's undergarments without express permission of the other teenager." You busted her bra strap, Jeff. Her *training* bra strap.

I didn't bust it.

I saw the undergarment. I thought with all that boat building, you'd have developed finer motor skills.

She said I could go to second base after the dance.

What have I told you about baseball metaphors for sex?

She told me I could feel her up after the dance.

The dance wasn't over. You were still on school property. You were still in the *building.* You attacked her in front of the testaments to our alma mater's finest athletic achievements. The state badminton first-place trophy of nineteen-fifty-eight, for example. You tried to feel her up in front of the Bronze Birdie. Have you no shame?

No one was looking.

That is not a sound legal defense, Woollypaws.

Oh, get off your high horse, will you? I didn't invent heavy petting, you know.

No, but you're making a career of it. With jailbait.

I'm jailbait.

You can say that again. Don't forget to call me when they finally lock you up.

I'm going over there.

A brilliant idea, and in keeping with most of your ideas regarding girls, such as "Never take no for an answer," "'No' means 'yes,'" "'Leave me alone' means 'Come right over.'"

Maybe that's what she wants. Maybe she's playing hard to get.

No, I think she's playing "Stay away from me or I'll sic my Doberman pinscher on you."

She has a golden retriever. Bonnie would never hurt me.

Oh, sigh.

I'm going over there. Want to come with me?

Whatever for?

She might talk to me with you there. And you could help me. You could tell me what to say.

Forget it, Woolleybrain. I will never be associating with you in person again.

Because of the Bicentennial Ball?

Oui.

But it was so long ago.

It was last month.

You really hold a grudge.

Assault victims tend to.

Assault? I kissed you.

Correction: You *tried* to kiss me.

Okay, *tried* to. So what?

You swore you wouldn't, that's what. You didn't have permission, that's what. You signed an affidavit stating that you wouldn't, that's what.

You looked like you wanted me to kiss you.

I was coming out of the little girls' room.

I really thought you wanted it.

You shouldn't think, Jeffrey. Or act. In fact, you should be muzzled. Those lips of yours are lethal weapons. With hair triggers.

You wanted it. You know you did.

I didn't, Jeffrey, and I know I didn't. I should have known better than to trust you. The only reason I went to the ball with you in the first place was because I pitied you.

***You* pitied *me*? That's a laugh.**

You couldn't find a date, remember? Dee dropped you the day of the ball. You begged me to go with you. Never mind that at school you act like I don't exist—

You mean *you* pretend *I* don't.

You exist, all right. You exist all over the place. Especially all over teenage girls.

Have you ever even kissed a guy?

Have you?

You're always handing out advice on the subject. What do you even know about it?

Nothing. And if I did, I wouldn't share it with the likes of you.

Just as I thought. You've never kissed anybody. I don't know why I listen to you.

I didn't say I'd never kissed anybody. I said I know nothing about it, and that I'm not willing to discuss my personal life with you.

That's the truth.

Meaning what?

**Meaning you never talk about your personal life
with me.**

You never ask.

**You never give straight answers. So I've had to find
other ways to find out what I want to know.**

What are you talking about?

**Well, for one thing, I noticed you went to the dance
tonight with Cornel Piedmont.**

We weren't hiding it.

Why didn't you tell me you were going together?

You never asked. And we're not going together. We
went to the dance together.

Did he try anything?

Yes, Jeffrey, he did. He tried his hardest not to laugh at
your, quote, *dancing*, unquote.

**You're the one who taught me to disco. At the ball,
remember?**

Don't blame me for your utter lack of rhythm and
grace.

And what about Cornel? He's got rhythm and grace? He looked like he was having seizures out there.

He was seized by fits of laughter watching you, especially when you broke into your air guitar solo during "Stairway to Heaven."

Shut up.

You even leaned backward and closed your eyes and scrunched up your face like Jimmy Page. I thought Cornel was going to have an aneurysm.

What do I care what he thinks? He's a dork. It doesn't make sense. You're so smart and he's so . . .

Yes?

Well . . .

I'm waiting.

Dumb, I guess.

He's written a novel.

A novel?

Uh-huh. It's about a planet where all the children are sent to prison, while the criminals are forced to serve their sentences in public school. The children are happier, of course. The criminals riot.

You're still too smart for him.

How do you define "smart"?

Getting straight As.

At Indianola, all you have to do to get As is show up, turn your assignments in on time, and suffer indignity in silence.

I can't believe you don't think you're smart. Everybody calls you a brain.

What a concept: calling someone by the organ they care most about. I wonder what they call you.

Ha, ha.

Intelligence isn't a penis, you know. It can't be measured.

Man, shut up!

What, you don't like girls to say "penis"?

No!

Penis, penis, penis, penis.

Stop it!

It's just a word. Like "basketball," or "vagina."

Will you cut it out?

For someone who thinks so much about sex, you're sure uncomfortable with the terminology.

Who says I think about it so much?

Do you own a puka shell choker?

What?

Do . . . you . . . own . . . a . . . puka . . . shell . . . choker?

Yeah, I do. So what?

When did you get it?

Why?

Just curious.

I don't know. Not too long ago.

After the ball?

I think so.

At the ball, just for fun, Tina Kasicki said very loudly to me at the punch bowl that guys with big penises tend to wear a lot of jewelry, especially necklaces. She added that really well-hung guys often prefer puka shell chokers. Two weeks later, the halls were choked with puka-shelled boys.

That's not why I bought it.

Of course it isn't.

It was a gift. From my aunt.

Right.

What were we talking about before you started—

Talking about penises? Or is it "peni"?

We were talking about you and your secrets.

I have no secrets. I have privacy.

Viv told me about your brother.

[CLICK]

[R-R-R-R-RING]

Caesar residence. At the tone, stab me in the back.

Did you take the phone off the hook?

I called Viv.

You didn't stay on very long.

I only said a couple words. Exactly two, in fact.

You should mellow out. It's not her fault.

The devil made her squeal?

She didn't squeal. We were talking and it just came out. Why didn't you tell me about your brother?

I was under the impression that as an American, I have the right to remain silent.

But I'm your friend.

So Viv seems to think.

I'm not your friend?

Define "friend."

Just answer.

I object, your honor. The prosecution is badgering the witness.

Are. We. Friends?

[silence]

Well?

Only on the phone.

[CLICK]

[R-R-R-R-RING]

Pet Rock Emporium. Ask about today's special on neutering.

What is your problem?

Got a mirror? I thought you were going over to Meg's.

You told me not to.

And that *worked*?

So far.

Then I'm telling you to stop sticking your nose into my beeswax.

It wasn't my fault. Viv told me. I can't stop her from talking, can I?

When did you two get reacquainted, anyway?

You said I should try to stay friends with my old girlfriends.

So you actually hear me sometimes?

Viv said your brother died in Nam. Is that true?

[CLICK]

[R-R-R-R-RING]

Barb and Dingbat's Extermination Service. Who
would you like dead?

What did I say *this* time?

I don't want to talk about it.

Which means you do.

Come again?

**You wouldn't say you didn't want to talk about it unless
you really wanted to talk about it.**

Is that so?

Absolutely.

Hmmm. You know what I think?

What?

I think you're full of bull crap.

You really don't want to talk about it?

I always say what I mean, Jeffrey.

Have it your way.

Whopper, hold the pickle.

I have a brother, you know.

Yes, I do: Tom.

He and my dad don't get along.

Your dad doesn't like his ponytail.

Or his sideburns. He doesn't show up here much anymore, but he writes me these long letters all about politics.

I know, Jeffrey. You've told me.

Tom says the government didn't care at all about the innocent people who died in Vietnam and Cambodia, or all the American guys who died or got their legs blown off and stuff.

That's what Tom says. What does Jeff say?

I don't know. I'm just glad the war's over. I was really scared I was going to get drafted.

Some people enlisted.

Crazy people.

Maybe they just believed in defending your freedom.

Tom says they all died for nothing.

A lot of people die for nothing.

What does that mean?

Nothing.

I'm just glad there's no more draft. You're so lucky you're a girl.

I remind myself of that every morning, just before I smear Nair on my lip.

So what's up with you and Viv?

Nair makes you think of Viv?

I guess so.

She does use the stuff by the truckload. Sometimes even on her legs.

You use it on your mustache. . . .

What's your point?

Viv said you guys aren't talking to each other.

We've grown apart. Like Sonny and Cher. She could never decide on eye shadow, and I could never decide which of the things she cares about these days is the most boring.

You guys have been friends a long time.

Since first grade.

She seems pretty upset.

Wonder why she chose to talk to you about it.

She wanted to know if me and you were going together. She saw us at the ball.

I bet. Did you tell her you'd lost a bet?

No. I told her we're just friends.

Did she see me knee you in the balls?

She was in the bathroom. She was mad she missed it.

Did she mention she keeps rubbers in her purse?

***Man,* Barb!**

She does.

Are you mad at her or me?

Six of one, half dozen of another.

What are you mad at Viv about?

My beeswax, Mr. Mammoth.

Does she really keep rubbers in her purse?

She's probably on the pill by now.

Viv's not like that.

No?

Remember, I used to go with her. She dropped me because I kissed her too much.

Did she?

Didn't she?

Believe what you want to believe. Believe what you *need* to believe.

You said she said I kiss like a maniac.

I didn't say she didn't like it.

***Did* she?**

No comment.

If she liked it, then why did she drop me?

She wasn't sure she wanted you to be the first, if you know what I mean, and I'm sure you do. She had her eye on someone else.

Who? Craig? She went with him after me. Did she do it with him?

Loyalty to my bosom buddy prevents me from saying. Aw, what the hell. We ain't so bosomy lately. Yeah, the hussy jumped him.

They sure didn't go together very long.

He got what he wanted, then moved on.

Is she going with anyone now?

Interested?

I don't know. . . .

Feeling lonely? Desperate? I mean, you've been girlfriendless for, what, an hour and a half?

Is she going with anyone or not?

You're gonna have to find that out yourself, from the whore's mouth.

Jesus, Barb. How can you talk about her like that? She was your friend.

She has a big mouth, and she doesn't use it exclusively for blabbing.

We mostly just talked about you.

That's comforting. Did she tell you I'm into voodoo now? I don't suppose you'd care to donate a lock of your hair and some fingernail clippings?

She told me you have a sister, too.

If you filled Viv's mouth with salt water, it would become the earth's eighth ocean.

What's your sister's name?

Barbara. My parents loved the name so much, they used it twice.

Come on, what's her name?

Balinda.

Balinda and Barbara?

Cute, huh?

Where does she live?

In a dorm at the U.

That's where my brother goes.

I know. Poli-sci major.

What's her major?

Education. Can't imagine why she'd want to be a teacher. I'd be an executioner first.

Is she married?

She's too old for you, Jeff. Plus she has the family excess-body-hair problem.

I'm just showing an interest.

In a female you've never met.

It was an innocent question.

No such thing.

Viv also told me about your mom. About being in a wheel—

[CLICK]

[R-R-R-R-RING]

Welcome to the Really Bad Advice Line. Here's our tip of the day: Pry into friends' personal lives. They'll love you for it.

Okay. I get it. I won't talk about your mom.

Good idea.

And I'm sorry about your brother.

Did you do it?

You know what I mean.

It was his own fault.

Why?

I don't want to talk about it.

You wanna talk about Meg instead?

He enlisted.

Because he enlisted, it's his fault he died? Maybe he signed up because he believed in the war.

The schlemiel.

Was he killed in action?

Schlemazel.

Jesus, Barb, your brother's dead and you're calling him *names*?

He was my brother. I'll call him what I like.

Viv said his name is Peter.

Viv is a schlemazel. His name *was* Paul. But I called him Pole.

Are you joking? I can never tell.

He was six-foot-five. I called him Pole.

When did he die?

He didn't.

Huh?

He was killed.

Okay, then, when was he killed?

No one knows for sure. Someone from the army called last June. The ninth. I was watching a rerun of *Andy Griffith*, the one where Opie gets accused of burning down a barn, though, of course, he didn't do it. Not our Opie. But his pa gave him a whuppin' anyway. Mom answered the phone in the kitchen. She screamed, and then I heard the receiver bounce off the floor. That's what I remember: the sound of Mom screaming, the phone hitting the linoleum, and canned laughter.

But the war ended in nineteen-seventy-three. All our troops were pulled out.

Not all of 'em. They left Pole behind.

You're kidding.

I'm kidding?

When did he go missing?

The sixteenth of March, nineteen-seventy-two.

You didn't know if he was alive or dead for three years?

I didn't realize you were such a math whiz. Three and a quarter years, actually. Mom watched the war on TV constantly, the body bags coming off the planes, hoping he wasn't in one of them. . . .

[silence]

I don't want to talk about her.

Right. Barb . . .

[silence]

. . . You don't have any TVs at your house.

I'm sorry?

You don't. I saw. I—I was there.

Here? When?

The night of the ball. I tried calling, but you'd taken the phone off the hook.

You came *here*?

Yeah. Your dad answered the door. He invited me in. Your mom was there, too. Viv's right. She's in a wheel—

[CLICK]

[R-R-R-R-RING]

St. Barbara's Catholic Church and Nursery School. Start confessing at the beep, but I can tell you right now your penance is ten Hail Marys and an Our Father.

I'm Methodist.

Do the penance anyway. A person like you could never do too much.

Your dad said he wasn't sure if you were home and I should check to see if you were in your room. Your room's over the garage.

Really?

You didn't answer when I knocked, so I went in.

You went in?

I just kind of peeked around, looking for you.

You thought I might be hiding?

No . . .

Did you rifle through my drawers? Did you fondle my underwear?

Shut up.

Did you find my shrunken head collection? Care to make a donation?

I saw a lot of bookshelves. On one shelf I saw a picture of a soldier in a frame. Is that Pole?

I should call a cop. You're a felon.

Don't be so melodramatic.

You broke and entered.

There was no TV in your room.

It was struck by lightning. It's in the shop.

There wasn't one in your living room, either.

It can strike twice, you know. It's rare, but it happens.

What's wrong with me seeing your mom in a wheelchair?

Ready to hear a dial tone?

Why is she in it? Is she sick?

She's lazy. Very, very lazy. That's why my dad bought it for her. He gave it to her for Mother's Day last year. Tied a big pink bow on it and everything. He's a very thoughtful guy, my dad.

Come off it.

Off what?

Just tell me. What's wrong with her?

If I tell you, will you keep it to yourself?

Uh-huh.

Promise?

Yes.

All right.

[silence]

She jumped into the rhino pen at the zoo and was gored.

That's not funny.

Who's laughing? I take rhinoceros attacks very seriously. You ever been involved in one?

Is there something wrong with her?

There's something wrong with everybody. You, for instance.

Is she sick or did she get hurt?

Hurt. Did you know they're made of matted hair?

What?

Rhinoceros horns.

Come on. Seriously. Is it that Jerry Lewis thing?

Idiocy?

Muscular whatever.

No, it was a muscular rhino and his horn of hair.

You never stop.

Bionic mouth. We couldn't afford the rest. I'm the six-*thousand*-dollar girl.

So you're not going to tell me?

I did tell you. You just can't handle it.

[silence]

Am I allowed to ask about your dad?

Why ask anything? Why talk at all? How 'bout I just go out for a couple hours and you drop by and break in and look for the answers you seek in my diaries. I'll leave them out for you, unlocked.

You're mad I came over.

You didn't "come over." You invaded.

I opened the door. I peeked in. I noticed things.

You *invaded*.

[CLICK]

[R-R-R-R-RING]

Central Intelligence Age—I mean, Capitol Plumbing Company.

Where is Dingbat? I didn't see her.

She was probably in another form. She's a familiar.

What's a familiar?

Look it up.

I'm sorry I looked in your room.

Broke in, you mean. Spied. Invaded.

So how do you know so much about TV if you don't have one? You know the shows and the theme songs and everything.

You said it yourself: It's all anyone ever talks about. And all my friends have TVs. Everybody has a TV.

Except you. Doesn't it make you feel left out?

Of what? I learn all I need to know just hanging out in the halls listening to vidiots like you.

Like me?

You watch TV nonstop.

What are you talking about?

You're not the only spy in town, Jeffrey.

What's that mean?

One . . . two . . . three . . . four . . . five . . .

You came to *my* house?

Bingo.

Was I home?

You were. I watched TV with you for a while.

How? Through the window?

Yes. And not just once.

That's illegal!

So call a cop.

You've been *spying* on me.

You're one to talk.

You're a Peeping Tom!

And you're a liar. And a housebreaker. And a vidiot. Not to mention a big, fat hypocrite. All your hot air about TV and you watch it just as much as anyone else, if not more.

What about all your hot air about how much you love it and your family doesn't even *own* one? You said you were watching *Andy Griffith* when the army called about your brother, and you said your mom watched the war on TV all the time, but—

[CLICK]

[R-R-R-R-RING]

Meow.

I get it.

Meow?

You guys got rid of your TVs, right? Because of your mom. So she'd stop watching.

Hello? Who's calling, please?

Cut it out, Barb.

Oh, it's you, Jeffrey. You've been talking to my cat, you know. *Bad* cat, Dingbat. *Bad* cat. No answering the phone. Go lie down. Go on. Sorry, Jeffrey. She's so uppity lately.

Did you get rid of your TVs because of your mom?

Dad smashed them. It was pretty cool to watch. I got to wear safety goggles and everything.

Viv says your mom had a nervous breakdown. Because of your brother.

[CLICK]

[R-R-R-R-RING]

White House Pardon Hotline. President Ford is busy at the moment forgiving someone else. Please hold.

If you hang up again, I swear to God I won't call back.

[CLICK]

[R-R-R-R-RING]

You are not a man of your word.

What is the big deal? Why can't I talk about your mom? I know everything anyway. From Viv.

Everything can't be known, especially from Viv.

Your mom can't walk anymore because she had a nervous breakdown, right? I didn't know that could happen.

She'll walk again. But she'll never ski. Of course, she never could.

You make a joke out of everything.

Everything is a joke. For example: What's funnier than a dead baby?

Is this a real joke?

A dead baby in a clown costume.

You're sick.

Craig Seaman told that joke in the lunchroom and his goons all busted a gut. So who's sick?

I see what you mean. It's like Hawkeye on *M*A*S*H*. The only way he can put up with all the mangled bodies every day is by cracking jokes.

Laugh and the world laughs with you. Cry and I'll give you something to cry about.

Who said that?

Some comic on Johnny Carson.

But you don't have TV.

I once did.

So what do you do in your free time without TV?

I talk on the phone. I read. I write letters to my sister. I read letters from my sister. I play Scrabble with my parents. I depilate.

What's "depilate"?

Look it up.

You play Scrabble with your parents?

I do. You have a problem with that?

Just the three of you?

I actually quite like my parents. They're decent and clean, and they let me have my own phone.

I never hang out with my parents. All they do is watch TV, anyway.

Like you.

So why do you live over the garage?

Because my brother bought the farm.

It was his room?

You're so quick.

Isn't it creepy sleeping in there?

Why would it be?

Well, it was his room, and he's dead. . . .

Do you believe in ghosts?

No, not really.

I do.

Have you ever, y'know . . . *seen* your brother?

Lots of times.

So why don't you move back to the house?

Because I like seeing him.

That's weird, man.

I'm weird, man.

[silence]

I'm going to Meg's. I know she'll listen to reason.

Maybe. But she won't hear any from you.

Bye, Barb. Thanks for nothing.

Anytime.

[CLICK]

[R-R-R-R-RING]

Yeah?

Jeff? It's me. Meg.

No, it isn't.

Pardon me?

First you're Dingbat, now you're Meg. I'm not in the mood for your head-tripping, Barb.

Barb? No, Jeff, it's *me*, Meg. You know. Your ex-girlfriend.

Oh yeah? Prove it.

Prove it?

Tell me something Barb wouldn't know.

You're real mad at me, aren't you, Jeff? Well, I don't think that's at all fair. I mean, I didn't put my hand up *your* dress.

Prove it or I hang up.

I like it when you're forceful like this, Jeff. On the phone, anyway. Okay, let me think. Hmmm, let me see. . . . Oh, I know! You kiss like a maniac!

[CLICK]

[R-R-R-R-RING]

Barb and Dingbat's Twenty-Four-Hour Make-Out Tips. What base are you on?

I called Meg.

Oh, *hi*, Jeff. What a pleasant surprise! I assumed you had left for Meg's.

Her phone's still off the hook. *You* called and pretended to be her. This is fun to you, isn't it? You like it when girls drop me. You're still mad about the pool thing. And the ball. This is revenge.

And it is sweet.

I've apologized to you about a zillion times. What are you still sore about?

Sore? Well, let's see. A boy is supposed to meet a girl at a public swimming pool but somehow ends up making out with a different girl behind a vending machine.

When, later, Girl A reveals this to him, the boy proceeds to call her by Girl B's name. The boy then takes it upon himself to use Girl A as his own personal Dear Abby, calling her whenever he has girl trouble, which is, of course, often. Then, after forgiving the boy and accompanying him to a dance, the boy breaks his solemn oath and violates Girl A. Does this sound like a boy who has learned from his mistakes? Does this sound like a boy who's sorry?

But you said you'd help me with girls.

I had no idea how much you didn't know. For example, I trusted I was wrong when I judged you to be a male chauvinist pig.

I hear that word a lot, but I don't exactly know what it means.

It's a fat barnyard animal that goes "oink"—or a fatheaded boy who does.

I mean "chauvinist."

Oh. That's a person who believes some people are better than others. A male chauvinist is a guy who thinks guys rule. He thinks girls are just here to smell nice, put out, have babies, and change diapers, in that order. Then it's cooking, cleaning, and keeping cold beer in the fridge till they die. We're also good nurses, teachers, and live nude dancers.

I don't think guys rule.

That's a start.

I respect girls.

That's . . . debatable.

I've had enough of this. I mean it. You think you can cut me down as much as you like, but you can't. I don't deserve it, and I'm not going to take it anymore. I don't care what you say, I'm going over to Meg's now, so don't bother calling back, because I won't be here.

Gee, Jeff. I'll miss you.

[CLICK]

[R-R-R-R-RING]

Barb and Dingbat's Automated I-Told-You-So Service.
Maybe next time you'll listen.

She didn't come out.

You're kidding.

I even threw pebbles at her window.

How romantic. Break anything?

Her dad came out and yelled at me in his pajamas.

What were you doing in his pajamas?

Ha, ha.

What'd you do?

**I took off. I ran all the way home. That's how freaked
out I was. Then I called her.**

That's my brave, stupid Jeffrey. What was the result?

Her dad picked up and said if I called again, he'd need to speak with my parents.

He's our county prosecutor, you know.

I won't call back.

Bright boy.

I don't get it. What did I do that was so bad? Why did she drop me?

You're right. You don't get it.

Get what?

Exactly.

I did everything you said. I listened to her. I tried to care about what she cared about. I didn't kiss her all the time. I even went to parties with her. And I didn't mind any of it all that much. I like her. She's funny and really sweet, and she's into boats, too, like me. She doesn't make models, but she used to live in Florida, and her dad had a catamaran, and she and him used to go sailing a lot.

[silence]

I don't want to break up with her.

She broke up with you.

I know. But I'm sure I can get her back. What do you think I should I do? Send her a note?

"Dear Meg, I'm sorry for mauling you. Will you still let me go to second base? Yes or no. Circle one. Sincerely, Jeff."

No, not that kind. A real letter. You could help me write it.

Jeffrey, this is not the end of the world. You're just a teenager. Did you think you two were going to get married?

[silence]

Oh, come *on*. Did you really?

I just thought maybe we could go out for a while. Longer than three weeks, anyway.

Long enough to get in her pants.

Shut up. I thought she loved me.

Did she ever say so?

No. But I could tell.

Like you could tell I wanted to kiss you?

No . . .

Did you tell her you love her?

No.

Why not?

**I'm not sure I do. I'm not that . . . I'm not very
attracted to her.**

No?

**You said it yourself once. She has the body of a
nine-year-old.**

So why'd you ask her out in the first place?

**I knew her from games and pep rallies and stuff. She
was always really nice to me. I thought maybe it'd be a
good idea to go with a girl who didn't drive me crazy
with her bod for a change. I thought maybe I should
go with someone nice and fun and not so foxy.**

So you liked her, you weren't attracted to her, yet you
mauled her anyway. You call that respect?

I didn't maul her.

Okay, you *attacked* her.

I *kissed* her, Barb.

You did a lot more than that, buddy. You slid your hand up her party dress. You tried to feel her up. And she doesn't even have breasts yet.

How do you know?

I repaired her training bra. Honestly, Dingbat has a bigger pair. Four pairs, actually.

I just got carried away. Don't you ever get carried away?

She asked you to stop.

Did she?

That's what she says.

I don't remember.

She does. You don't know what "don't" means, do you?

Of course I do.

No you don't.

I do.

You don't.

[silence]

Okay, maybe I don't. I mean, I *do*, but I—I don't know. I forget when I'm feeling . . .

Amorous?

What's that?

Horny.

Oh. I guess so.

What are you gonna do about it?

Do?

How are you going to learn to "don't"?

I thought girls wanted it as much as guys do. The sexual revolution and all that.

We do when we do. We don't when we don't. When we don't, you can't. That's the revolution.

Did Cornel try to kiss you?

And whether we do or don't is our own beeswax.

I bet if I wait awhile, her dad will go to sleep.

You are insane. Someone has to stop you. I guess the duty falls to me. Jeffrey, you are *not* to leave your room. Consider this a citizen's arrest. A citizen's *house* arrest. You are grounded, mister. Where are your parents, anyway? Don't they exercise any control over you? You can just come and go as you please?

Yeah. Parents are different when it comes to guys. Less uptight. My curfew's midnight on weekends. They never even ask where I'm going.

It's after eleven-thirty.

I'm sure they're asleep. Besides, I came in after one once and they didn't even notice.

How nice that your parents don't notice you.

They trust me.

The county prosecutor doesn't.

I'm sure he's asleep by now, too.

Don't do it, Jeffrey. I know you don't know what "don't" means, but don't. Try to put Meg out of your mind. There will be other girls.

I'm going.

Then I'm going to call her and warn her.

Her dad will answer.

Then I will tell him there's a madman on his way over and to man his battle station.

You wouldn't do that. You wouldn't get me in trouble on purpose. Would you?

I would.

You would not.

I will.

You won't.

[silence]

Will you?

Try me.

[silence]

Okay.

[CLICK]

[R-R-R-R-RING]

Barb and Dingbat's Bail Bonds. What did you do now?

Where's Dingbat?

Come again?

Dingbat. Where is she?

You want to speak with her?

Answer the question.

Why do you want to talk to Dingbat again? Are you hitting on *her*? You are aware that she isn't human, aren't you? Then again, that probably doesn't matter to you.

I didn't go to Meg's.

Bravo. I'm proud of you.

I was on my way there, but then I got nervous you'd really call and Meg's dad would be there waiting for me.

I didn't call.

Why not?

I didn't need to.

Why?

You didn't go, did you?

I could go now.

Is that your plan?

Maybe.

But it's after midnight. Past your curfew. And Valentine's Day is over.

My dad heard me come in. He met me in the hall. He smiled and asked me if I got any.

Any what?

You know.

Yes, I do. I just can't handle it. The pervert doesn't fall far from the tree.

What's that supposed to mean?

Like father, like son.

You're calling my dad a pervert?

Not explicitly.

My dad's just like any other guy.

Any other guy who encourages teen sex. How would he feel if you were a girl and guys were already trying to get into your pants?

I don't know. Maybe you should ask him.

I doubt he'd be happy about his daughter going with guys like you who have dads like him.

Did you go to bed?

No.

What have you been doing?

I gave Dingbat a bath.

You gave your *cat* a *bath*?

Yes. *Thpppt! Thpppt!* Stupid fur!

Wait—you licked her clean?

No, Jeffrey. It's a joke. I gave her a normal bath, with soap and water. And, like always, she threw a hissy fit when the tiniest bit of shampoo got in her eyes. She is such a big kitten.

You're lying.

Oh yeah? You wanna see the scratches on my arm? Did you know cats have venom in their claws? That's why their scratches sting.

You did not give Dingbat a bath.

You're too sharp for me. That was a joke, too. Cats bathe themselves.

I was there.

You were where?

After I changed my mind about going to Meg's, I went to your house. I watched you through your window.

Are you stalking me?

I didn't see Dingbat.

That's because you were probably looking for a cat. She's been in the form of a gnat all night.

Shut up.

Okay, then how about this: She's buried in the yard.

She's dead?

Well, I wouldn't bury her alive.

When did she die?

When I was seven.

She been dead all this time?

No, she's risen a couple times. Dingbat the zombie cat.

So she wasn't there the night you called me about Viv?

Actually, I've never owned a cat.

Never?

I'm allergic.

[silence]

Tell me one true thing you've ever said to me, Barb. Just one. Because right now I think you do nothing but lie.

I do nothing but utter the gospel truth,
Mr. Woolworth.

Which is a lie.

I told you Cornel wrote a novel. That was true. He's calling it *Little Kids in the Big House*.

No he didn't.

All right. You caught me in a little fib. It's a novella.

Bull crap.

Well, he *intends* to write it. He has an outline. And the title. And the price.

Did Meg really show up at your house tonight?

Yes.

Liar.

How else could I know you molested her?

Maybe you saw us.

The Bronze Birdie Bra Strap Attack? I think I'd remember.

That's why you don't want me to go over to her house, because she'd tell me she didn't go to *your* house. I bet she didn't break up with me at all. You made it all up.

I did?

I'm going to call her tomorrow and ask.

She won't talk to you. She'll hang up if you call.

You are such a liar.

Am not.

Are too.

Am not, infinity.

How can you even pretend you tell the truth after I've caught you in so many lies?

What else can a liar say? If I admit I was a liar, I'd be telling the truth. And then I would be a liar.

So you admit it.

Absolutely not. I cannot tell a lie.

What about your brother?

What about him?

Was he really killed in Vietnam?

Ask the army.

You told me he was. You told Viv he was. Was he or wasn't he?

If you say I'm a liar, what can I say that you'd believe?

At this point, nothing.

Then I'll say that.

What about your mom?

What about her?

If your brother wasn't killed, then why is she in a wheelchair?

I told you. Rhinoceros attack.

And why no TVs if he wasn't killed?

Lightning. Two bolts. Remember? Zap. Zap.

And that day at the pool?

What about it?

Who did I really kiss behind the Coke machine?

You don't know?

Was it you?

Was it?

Why are you doing this to me?

Doing what?

Driving me crazy.

Short drive.

But *why*?

Because I can. It's not my fault you can't keep track of your victims.

"Victims"? Meg is my "victim"?

And Dee. And Marla. And Pammi. And Tina. Not to mention me.

Just exactly what did I do to them?

You treated *us* as objects.

Cut the women's lib bull crap. Why don't you burn your bra while you're at it?

I don't wear one. I don't need one. Why don't you stop busting them?

How did I treat you guys as "objects"?

You tried to kiss me when I told you not to. You kissed Dee thinking it was me. You pressured Marla to let you feel her up. You mauled Meg. Need I say more?

You act like I'm some kind of *pervert* or something.

A pervert and a Peeping Tom.

You peeked in *my* windows.

Did I?

Didn't you?

I didn't.

You said you did.

Did I?

If you didn't watch me through the window, how'd you know what shows I watched?

One . . . two . . . three . . . four . . .

Meg?

And Viv. And Marla and Pammi and Tina.
Apparently, you liked to lure them into your room
for heavy petting.

So you lied again. You didn't come over here. You didn't spy on me.

Yes, Jeffrey, I'm guilty of respecting your privacy.
How about you? What did you see tonight on your
prowlings?

Uh . . . well . . . I saw . . .

[silence]

You saw what?

You know.

No, I don't, Jeffrey. What did you see?

You know what you were doing. I saw . . . that.

[CLICK]

[R-R-R-R-RING]

Perverts Anonymous. Keep it to yourself.

Did you take the phone off the hook? The line was busy forever.

I was chatting with a nice police officer. She asked me a lot of questions. She said someone will be dropping by your place very soon. You might want to pack an overnight bag.

You didn't call the fuzz. You wouldn't do something that low.

No? Wait and see.

Look, I'm sorry. I didn't do it on purpose.

You accidentally peered in my window?

I didn't mean to *see* you. I just peeked in to see if you were awake. I didn't know you'd be . . .

What?

You know.

No, I don't. Tell me.

I saw you. In your bed. Under the covers. In the dark.

You saw me in the dark? Do you have infrared vision
or something? Are you a superhero?

**I saw you . . . you know . . . I didn't mean to. I'm sorry I
saw it. Really. And as soon as I saw what you were
doing, I left. I didn't do anything wrong. Except
maybe peek in the window. But I was just checking to
see if you were awake or not. I swear I'll never tell
anyone.**

I appreciate your candor, Jeffrey. I don't know *why* you
felt you must tell me what you saw, but it's better than
you telling everyone in town, I guess. If you solemnly
swear on your little toy boats, I'll admit what I was
doing.

You don't need to tell me. God! Let just forget it.

No, I feel I must come clean.

***Please* don't. I'd rather pretend I never saw it.**

I was—

Don't say it!

Knitting.

What? *Knitting?*

Yes. And I'm not ashamed to admit it.

That's *not* what you were doing.

There's nothing wrong with knitting, Jeffrey. People have been knitting for centuries. Especially female people.

You weren't knitting. The lights were out.

I like knitting in the dark. I concentrate better.

Oh, come *on*.

Lots of people knit in the dark, Jeff. Helen Keller, for instance. And Stevie Wonder.

But they're *blind*.

Blind, yes, but exceptional needleworkers.

Stevie Wonder?

Apparently, music has always been his *second* greatest

passion. Knitting is his first love, or so he said in an interview in *Knit* magazine last year. I subscribe. He was on the cover, in fact, wearing a lovely chenille sweater he knitted. I think it was the October issue. I can check if you like.

But he's a *guy*.

Your sexism is showing, Jeffrey. One shouldn't stereotype. Tough guys can do needlework. David Carradine knits, for example.

The guy on *Kung Fu*?

That's right. So does Kareem Abdul-Jabbar, and Jimmy Page. Jimmy says knitting helps him relax backstage before a gig.

Now I know you're lying. Jimmy Page does not *knit*.

I keep my back issues. I'm happy to lend.

You weren't knitting, Barb.

How do you know? It was dark.

It wasn't *that* dark. And your hands were under the covers.

[silence]

All right, Jeffrey. You've caught me dead to rights. If you swear again to keep it to yourself, I'll admit what I was *really* doing.

I really don't want you to. Jesus, can't you just drop the whole thing?

I was crocheting.

Crocheting?

No knitter with any self-respect wants to get caught crocheting. That's why I only do it late at night with the lights out, and "undercover," so to speak.

You weren't crocheting.

No? What do you think I was doing?

Never mind.

Don't you ever knit in the dark in the privacy of your own room, Jeffrey? Or are you a crocheter? You're not a needlepointer, are you? I bet you're a needlepointer. I bet you point your needle all the livelong day.

So I guess this means you get horny, too.

What does?

Knitting in the dark.

I don't see the connection.

Do you get horny or not?

Doesn't everybody? Except my parents, of course.

Are you still a virgin?

That is not your beeswax. That is *my* beeswax. For the last time, stay away from it.

Do you think it's wrong for me to want to go all the way?

No, it isn't wrong. To want to.

But to *do* it is, right?

It's how little babies get made, you know, Jeffrey. Not to mention how VD gets spread.

You sound like one of those commercials that come on real late at night.

"This has been a public service announcement paid for by People Against Horny Teenagers Going All the Way. The views expressed in this announcement do not necessarily reflect those of this television station, especially considering we show *Welcome Back, Kotter*, which does sort of make teen sex seem pretty cool."

So how long should I wait, then? Till I'm twenty?

When you can snatch the pebble from my hand, Grasshopper, you will be ready to go all the way. Till that time, stick with needlepoint.

Sounds like Viv snatched the pebble. She must have been ready.

Viv was not ready. She was *randy*, like you. My advice, Grasshopper, is never make an important decision while randy.

Cut the *Kung Fu* bull crap, okay?

David Carradine knits, remember? It is nothing to be ashamed of. It will only make you go blind if you do it for years and years under inadequate lighting.

Don't bring all that up again. Look, I'm beat. I'm going to bed. It's been a hairy night.

I think that is a wise decision, Grasshopper. Think not of your many transgressions. This is a time of great change. Rest in peace.

I wish I could give you a kung fu chop.

That is just your youthful exuberance speaking. In time you will see that martial arts are not about inflicting pain, but rather—

You know what I think?

How could I possibly?

I think you're chicken.

You think I'm what?

Chicken.

Well, that's just about the nicest thing anyone's ever said to me, Jeff. Blucks a lot.

The reason you only talk to me on the phone is because you're too chicken to tell me off in person. You can't tell me to my face what's bugging you. You have to hide in your room, behind your phone.

Really? And here I thought it was because confronting you to your face usually leads to getting confronted *by* your face.

You hide behind your sarcasm, too. You're afraid to say what you really think. Or feel. You just take cheap shots and then pretend you're kidding. I wonder if even *you* know when you're telling the truth.

What is truth anyway?

Shut up already. You seem to think you can say

whatever you want to me, like you owe it to me. Does it make you feel any better to keep putting me down, or making fun of everything I say, or playing all kinds of games? You say you want to help me, but I don't think you do. I think you just want to keep twisting the knife so that I'll keep apologizing. But you're a chicken. You're not even brave enough to do it in person. You can't look me in the eye and call me a jerk.

I kneed you in the balls. Wasn't that brave?

Yeah, it was. At least I really knew what you felt. You were pissed. And you showed it.

So you want to come over and I'll do it a couple more times?

Sure, I'll come over, and you can give me your best shot. I can take it. Let me have it, about everything. About the pool and Dee and trying to kiss you at the ball and Meg and invading your privacy and everything. If you're still too angry after that to be friends, then let's just forget about it. But no more long phone calls. I'm sick of them. They drive me crazy.

Shor—

"Short drive," I know. Ha, ha.

[silence]

You're right.

I am? About what?

Everything.

"Everything can't be known." Isn't that what you said?

I am a coward. You're right. I wasn't brave enough to introduce myself to you. Tina had to set us up. I wasn't brave enough to walk over and slap your face at the pool, which is what you deserved.

I did, and you definitely should have. It would have been better than stewing over it for months. Or playing mean games over the phone just to get me back. Sticking pins in a voodoo doll.

So you liked it more when I kneed you in the nuts?

Yeah, even though it hurt like hell.

It hurt like hell when you kissed Dee, too. And when you tried to kiss me when I told you not to. And when you kissed all those girls without caring one bit who they were or what they wanted.

You really are pissed at me. Maybe I really should come over so you can bite my head off.

No.

Why not?

I'm not allowed to have boys in my room without permission. Maybe later.

You might not feel as brave later.

How about for brunch?

Brunch?

My dad makes a big breakfast on Sunday mornings. Waffles. Eggs. Fruit salad. The works. Why don't you come over?

For brunch? With you and your dad?

And my mom.

You want me to come over and eat waffles with you and your parents?

Yes. Just as if you were a real person.

Are you going to bite my head off right in front of them?

No. I don't think I need to anymore. Just hearing you say you deserve it was enough. I don't feel as angry all of a sudden.

My foot. You've got something up your sleeve. Some sort of clever revenge. Like maybe inviting Meg to brunch, too. And Viv. And maybe Pammi and Marla and Tina. Then you guys could all gang up on me.

No. I'll have to be nice to you. My parents will make me.

Bull crap. You're up to something.

After we eat and do the dishes, we usually all sit down together for a game of Scrabble. "The family that plays together," etcetera.

I suck at Scrabble.

Fabulous. I'll trounce you.

Sounds like a real gas.

You can ask my mom or dad if I've been lying to you about my brother's death. They'll tell you. They're adults. They're not allowed to lie about such serious topics.

You want me to ask your parents if their son was killed in Vietnam or not?

The direct approach is always best.

Can I ask your mom why she's in a wheelchair?

If you feel you must, but I'll tell you now that Viv was right: She had a nervous breakdown because of Pole. You can also ask my dad about Meg. He answered the door when she rang the bell tonight.

None of this sounds like fun to me.

You got something better to do?

I was supposed to go over to Meg's.

Well, that's off. So you'll come?

I don't trust you.

I don't trust you, either. That's why I want my parents around. My dad is big and tough. And he has a chainsaw. He won't tolerate any shenanigans.

Shenanigans?

Mauling. Rude kissing. Bra busting.

[silence]

What time should I come over?

Early. Ten.

Ten's early?

If I could, I'd sleep till noon every day.

Me too. If not later.

Adults don't understand how exhausting puberty is.

Yeah.

Brunch then?

Why don't I just come over now?

Brunch, Woolley. At ten. Final offer.

All right, but if something better comes up, I'm going to call and cancel.

You do and it will be the last time you will *ever* hear my voice on the telephone.

Promises, promises.

It's not a promise. It's a threat.

Okay, okay, I won't cancel.

You don't have to bring anything, though flowers would be nice. For Mother, I mean. She likes gardenias.

You want me to bring *flowers*?

I'm just saying gardenias would be a thoughtful gift. They cheer Mother up.

Okay, okay. Gardenias. What color?

They're usually white.

How many?

Use your own judgment. It would also be nice of you to bring some fruit. For the brunch. And I don't mean bananas. Something exotic. A pineapple would be perfect.

A pineapple?

Don't you want to make a good first impression?

I guess. . . .

Oh! You should also bring something for Dingbat. She loves treats. Sardines are her favorite.

Dingbat? But you said—

Gardenias, a pineapple, and a can of sardines. Got it, Jeffrey?

No, I don't get it. I don't get you. I don't know what you're up to. A little while ago you said you called the fuzz on me for looking in your window. Now you're

inviting me to *brunch*? And you want me to bring your cat sardines when you've never even had a cat? I don't get you.

You're right. You don't. But you can have waffles with me, so long as there is parental supervision.

I'll bring the flowers and the pineapple. But no sardines.

That's your call, but, remember, cat scratches are venomous.

Yeah, yeah, okay.

[silence]

Say, Barb . . .

What is it, Grasshopper?

I was just wondering . . .

[silence]

Do not be afraid, my son.

Will you cut that out?

Sorry.

You said Viv made it with Craig and that they broke

up, but you didn't say if she was going with anybody new or not.

Right, I didn't.

Do you think she's still up?

Oh, meow.

[CLICK]

While in junior high, **Patrick Jennings**'s girlfriend asked a friend to call him and drop him for her. He thought writing a book about this traumatic event might help him get over it. He was wrong.

Patrick's critically acclaimed Ike and Mem series was published by Holiday House. His most recent young adult novel, *Wish Riders*, was hailed by *The Horn Book* as "startlingly original." *Barb & Dingbat's Crybaby Hotline* is his thirteenth book. Read about his others, and meet his cats, at www.patrickjennings.com.